The Last Green Leaf

CARON WYKLE

PAGE PUBLISHING, INC.
Conneaut Lake, PA

First originally published by Page Publishing 2020

ISBN 978-1-64701-207-6 (hc)
ISBN 978-1-64701-206-9 (digital)

Printed in the United States of America

Acknowledgment

Thank you to my mother, who is an avid reader, for her love and encouragement, my friends and family, and to Noah Hrbek for the beautiful illustrations.

Spring had arrived, and all the bare trees were starting to bud their little, tiny leaves. Some trees had green buds that blossomed into pretty flowers, some white and some pink.

This particular tree bloomed white flowers, and as time passed, the flower petals fell off and tiny, little leaves were revealed.

There was one leaf in particular who was eager to make his appearance. His name was Petey. Petey loved the way the sun touched his face and when the rain would fall because he knew that was going to make him grow.

All of Petey's leafy friends were super excited. They talked about the birds and squirrels who lived in their tree, not forgetting the ladybugs, caterpillars, and noisy woodpeckers.

He loved listening to the birds sing and the little chirps coming from the newly hatched baby birds, waiting for their moms and dads to bring them food.

One day, Rita, the ladybug, paid him a visit. He liked it when she visited. She would always update him on the latest news of things happening in other trees and on the ground.

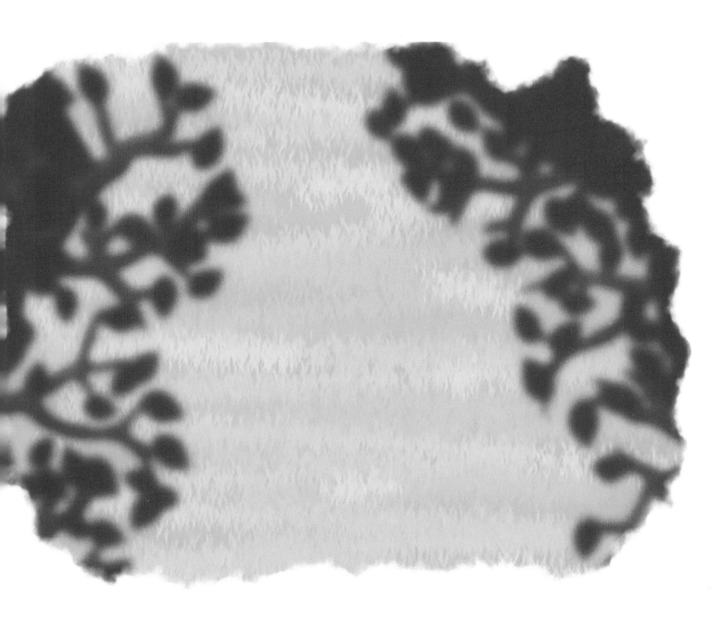

The ground was a great mystery to him. There was a lot of green as far as the eye could see and colorful flowers in bloom. He always wondered what it would be like down there.

Well, spring turned into summer, and Mr. Caterpillar told Petey that he was preparing for a trip and that when he comes back, he will be a beautiful butterfly.

Petey thought about when he would change. All his leafy friends said that when the weather changes and the wind and rain get cold, that's when they will change into fall colors. They also said some will be vibrant reds, orange, and yellow or a combination of colors.

They were excited because it meant that some special human child would pick them up after they have fallen from the trees to the ground.

So, as summer passed, the weather began to change, and Petey noticed some of his friends starting to change colors. They were happy, waving about in the wind.

Petey also noticed that he was not changing colors. He was still green. He asked his parents why he had not changed colors yet. His Mother said, "Don't worry, dear. It will happen soon."

The days and weeks passed and still no change. Many of his friends were already on the ground, being picked up by giggling little children.

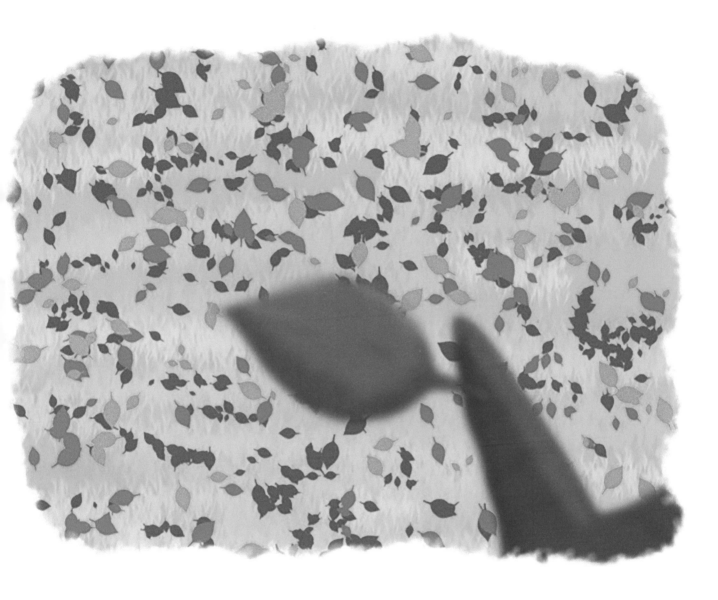

Then one day, he looked around and he was the only one left on the tree that was green. Petey was very sad because he was still green.

All of a sudden, a really strong wind started to blow. He waved about to and fro, and then it happened. He was released from the tree. He gently floated down to the ground. The sun was shining brightly on this crisp fall day. Some of his colorful, leafy friends were anxiously awaiting giggling children to pick them up.

He heard laughter in the distance as the kids were picking up all the fall-colored leaves. But to his surprise, Petey looked up and a beautiful little girl was staring at him. She had the biggest smile on her face and was calling to her Mother to come and see.

She asked her Mother, "Oh please can I have this one because it's the only one that is still green?"

To the girl's delight, her Mother said yes. They picked Petey up and took him home where he was displayed in the cutest little picture frame, admired by the little girl and all her friends.

Petey was so happy that he was the last green leaf.

The End

About the Author

Caron Wykle grew up in Shaker Heights, Ohio. She was a very active child—she played the cello, sung in the a capella choir, and joined gymnastics, varsity cheerleading, and modern dance. As an adult, she has been performing in a musical theatre for a little over nineteen years. She is currently involved in ballroom  dancing where she competes and does dance showcases. She has a passion for interior decorating, does home remodeling, and loves to cook. She also works with an organization that interprets popular children's books through acting, singing, and dancing for inner city school kids and kids from homeless shelters. Caron started tapping into her own imaginations one day and decided to write them down on paper, which evolved into the *Last Green Leaf*.

CPSIA information can be obtained
at www.ICGtesting.com
Printed in the USA
BVHW020147291220
596643BV00008B/53